*Tradition unravels . . .*

*chaos results . . .*

*magic happens!*

# COMING
# OUT

## SISTERS

"Steel's plots are first-rate—and this one is no exception."
—*The Star-Ledger*

"Female bonding with a cozy slumber-party vibe."
—*Kirkus Reviews*

## H.R.H.

"A journey of discovery, change and awakening . . . a story of love found, love lost and ultimately an ending that proves surprising." —*Asbury Park Press*

"Steel's fans will be waiting for this one." —*Booklist*

## THE HOUSE

"Many happy endings." —*Chicago Tribune*

"A . . . Steel fairy tale." —*Booklist*

**A MAIN SELECTION OF THE LITERARY GUILD
AND THE DOUBLEDAY BOOK CLUB**

# DANIELLE STEEL

# COMING OUT

### A NOVEL

*A Dell Book*
NEW YORK

To my wonderful and very special children:
Beatrix, Trevor, Todd, Nick,
Samantha, Victoria, Vanessa,
Maxx, and Zara,
for all their courage and grace
as they grow up.
For the wisdom, laughter, and love
they share with me so lavishly.
With my thanks for all you have taught me,
about what matters in life, and
the precious times we share. May you be
forever blessed. With all my heart and love,

Mom/d.s

## Proverbs 31

10: Who can find a virtuous woman? For her price is far above rubies.

11: The heart of her husband doth safely trust in her....

12: She will do him good and not evil all the days of her life.

13: ...She worketh willingly with her hands.

14: ...She bringeth her food from afar.

15: She riseth while it is yet night, and giveth meat to her household....

16: She considereth a field and buyeth it: with the fruit of her hands she planteth a vineyard.

18: ...her candle goeth not out by night.

20: She stretcheth out her hand to the poor; yea, she reacheth forth her hands to the needy.

# COMING
# OUT

# Chapter 1

*Olympia Crawford Rubinstein* was whizzing around her kitchen on a sunny May morning, in the brownstone she shared with her family on Jane Street in New York, near the old meat-packing district of the West Village. It had long since become a fashionable neighborhood of mostly modern apartment buildings with doormen, and old renovated brownstones. Olympia was fixing lunch for her five-year-old son, Max. The school bus was due to drop him off in a few minutes. He was in kindergarten at Dalton, and Friday was a half day for him. She always took Fridays off to spend them with him. Although Olympia had three older children from her first marriage, Max was Olympia and Harry's only child.

Olympia and Harry had restored the house six years before, when she was pregnant with Max. Before that, from Munich at ten, and lost her entire family. His father had been one of the few survivors of Auschwitz, and they met in Israel later. They had married as teenagers, moved to London, and from there to the States. Both had lost their entire families, and their only son had become the focus of all their energies, dreams, and hopes. They had worked like slaves all their lives to give him an education, his father as a tailor and his mother as a seamstress, working in the sweatshops of the Lower East Side, and eventually on Seventh Avenue in what was later referred to as the garment district. His father had died just after Harry and Olympia married. Harry's greatest regret was that his father hadn't known Max. Harry's mother, Frieda, was a strong, intelligent, loving woman of seventy-six, who thought her son was a genius, and her grandson a prodigy.

Olympia had converted from her staunch Episcopalian background to Judaism when she married Harry. They attended a Reform synagogue, and Olympia said the prayers for Shabbat every Friday night, and lit the candles, which never failed to touch Harry. There was no doubt in Harry's mind, or even his mother's, that Olympia was a fantastic woman, a great mother to all her children, a terrific attorney, and a wonderful wife. Like Olympia, Harry had been married before, but he had no other children. Olympia was turning forty-five blood and aristocratic connections. She had just enough left to pay for her education, and put a small nest egg away, which later paid for law school.

She married her college sweetheart, Chauncey Bedham Walker IV, six months after she graduated from Vassar, and he from Princeton. He had been charming, handsome, and fun-loving, the captain of the crew team, an expert horseman, played polo, and when they met, Olympia was understandably dazzled by him. Olympia was head over heels in love with him, and didn't give a damn about his family's enormous fortune. She was totally in love with Chauncey, enough so as not to notice that he drank too much, played constantly, had a roving eye, and spent far too much money. He went to work in his family's investment bank, and did anything he wanted, which eventually included going to work as seldom as possible, spending literally no time with her, and having random affairs with a multitude of women. By the time she knew what was happening, she and Chauncey had three children. Charlie came along two years after they were married, and his identical twin sisters, Virginia and Veronica, three years later. When she and Chauncey split up seven years after they married, Charlie was five, the twins two, and Olympia was twenty-nine years old. As soon as they separated, he quit his job at the bank, and went to live in Newport wife and their children. To add insult to injury, he had forced Olympia to agree that she would never urge their children to become Jewish. It wasn't an issue anyway. She had no intention of doing so. Olympia's conversion was a private, personal decision between her and Harry. Chauncey was unabashedly anti-Semitic. Harry thought Olympia's first husband was pompous, arrogant, and useless. Other than the fact that he was her children's father and she had loved him when she married him, for the past fifteen years, Olympia found it impossible to defend him. Prejudice was Chauncey's middle name. There was absolutely nothing politically correct about him or Felicia, and Harry loathed him. They represented everything he detested, and he could never understand how Olympia had tolerated him for ten minutes, let alone seven years of marriage. People like Chauncey and Felicia, and the whole hierarchy of Newport society, and all it stood for, were a mystery to Harry. He wanted to know nothing about it, and Olympia's occasional explanations were wasted on him.

Harry adored Olympia, her three children, and their son, Max. And in some ways, her daughter Veronica seemed more like Harry's daughter than Chauncey's. They shared all of the same extremely liberal, socially responsible ideas. Virginia, her twin, was much more of a throwback to their Newport worlds, a career she loved and that satisfied her, and a family that was the hub and core of her emotional existence. Each seemed to enhance and complement the other.

Olympia was taking Max to soccer practice that afternoon. She loved her time at home with her children. The twins would be home later that day, after their own after-school activities, which in their case included softball, tennis, swimming, and boys, whenever possible, particularly in Virginia's case. Veronica was more standoffish, shyer like her mother, and extremely particular about who she hung out with. Officially, Virginia was more "popular," and Veronica the better student. Both girls had just been accepted at Brown for the fall, and were graduating in June.

Charlie had been accepted at Princeton, like his father, and three generations of Walkers before him, but had decided to go to Dartmouth instead, where he played ice hockey, and Olympia prayed that in spite of that he would graduate with teeth. He was due home for the summer in a week, and after visiting his father, stepmother, and three half-sisters in Newport, he was going to work at a camp in Colorado, teaching riding and taking care of horses. He had his father's love of equestrian pursuits, and was a skilled polo player, but preferred more informal aspects of the sport. Riding Western saddle all summer, and teaching kids, seemed with diapers and nursing schedules all over again. Those days were over for her, and having Max in their life, to bind them even closer together, seemed like an incredible gift.

Olympia ran to open the door as soon as she heard the bell, and there was Max, in all his five-year-old splendor, with a wide, happy grin, as he threw his arms around his mother's neck and hugged her, as he always did when he saw her. He was a happy, affectionate little boy.

"I had a *great* day, Mom!" he said enthusiastically. Max loved everything about life, his parents, his sisters, his brother whom he seldom saw but was crazy about, his grandmother, the sports he played, the movies he watched, the food his mother served him, his teachers, and his friends at school. "We had cupcakes for Jenny's birthday! They were chocolate with *sprinkles*!" He said it as though describing some rare and fabulous occurrence, although Olympia knew from volunteering in his kindergarten class that they had a birthday, with cupcakes and sprinkles, nearly every week. But to Max, every day, and the opportunities it offered, was wonderful and new.

"That sounds yummy." She beamed down at him, noticing the paint splattered all over his T-shirt. He dropped his sweatshirt on a chair, and she saw that his new tennis shoes were covered with paint, too.

her legal work. She did her best to keep her two worlds separate. She rarely talked about her work with her children, unless they asked her. At home, she was more interested in talking about what they were doing. And she only had a sitter for Max for the hours she was at work, and not a minute longer. She loved being with him, and savored their time together.

"How did you know we had art today?" Max asked with interest, as he bit into the turkey sandwich she had made him. She did it just the way he liked it, with the right amount of mayonnaise, and a heap of his favorite potato chips. Her motherly skills were finely honed, and four star as far as Max was concerned. Her husband and three other children agreed. She was a good cook, a devoted mother, and made herself available to listen to their woes and solve their problems. She knew most of everything they did. She never divulged secrets, and gave fairly good advice about romantic problems, or so Virginia said. Veronica usually kept her crushes to herself, as Charlie did. He kept his own counsel about his relationships at college, just as he had when he was at home and in school. Charlie was a discreet and very private person and always had been. Harry said he was a "mensch," a man of integrity and great value. Sometimes he said Olympia she still had Max to assure her that she could do no wrong. It was reassuring, and had been for the past couple of years, as the twins negotiated their way across the reefs and shoals of the teenage years. Particularly Virginia, who frequently disagreed with her mother, especially over things she wasn't allowed to do. Veronica's battles with her were over broader issues, and related more to the ills and injustices of the world.

Olympia felt that adolescent girls were a lot tougher to deal with than little boys in kindergarten, to say the least, or even their college junior brother, who had always been quiet, easy to get along with, and extremely reasonable. Charlie was the family negotiator and peacemaker, anxious to see that everyone got along, particularly the two branches of his extended family. He often saw both his mother's and his father's divergent points of view and ran interference between them, and when one of his sisters had an argument with their mother, it was Charlie who translated and negotiated the peace. Veronica was the acknowledged hothead and rebel, with some occasionally dicey political points of view, and Virginia was the fluff in the family, according to her twin sister. Virginia was usually more concerned with her looks and her love life than with deeper social or political issues. Veronica and Harry engaged in long, lief. It was finally spring. The warmer weather always took too long to come, as far as she was concerned. She hated the long eastern winters. By May, she was sick to death of warm coats, boots, snowsuits, mittens, and random snowstorms that came out of nowhere in April. She could hardly wait for the summer and their trip to Europe. She, Max, and Harry were going to the south of France for two weeks before they met the girls in Venice. By then, she'd be ready to escape the torrid summer heat in New York. Max was going to day camp until they left, where he could do art projects to his heart's content.

The remains of Max's grape juice Popsicle were dripping copiously down his chin and onto his shirt as he ate the cookie, while his mother glanced at the last piece of mail in the stack, and set down her iced tea. It was a large ecru-colored envelope that looked like a wedding invitation, and she couldn't imagine a single person they knew who might be getting married. She tore it open as Max began to hum a song he had learned in school, just as she saw that it was not a wedding invitation, but an invitation to a ball that was to take place in December, a very special ball. It was an invitation to the very elite debutante cotillion where she had come out herself at eighteen. It was called The Arches, after the elegant name and design of the Astor estate where it had originally been held. The estate evening, and although admittedly somewhat old-fashioned and elitist, it did no one any harm. Olympia still cherished fond memories of her own debut, and had always assumed that her daughters would make their debut as well.

She had it in perspective, and knew how unimportant it was in the real scheme of things and world events, but also how much fun it could be for the girls who did it. It was a harmless even if frivolous landmark in a girl's life. She also knew that Chauncey expected the girls to do it, and would have been horrified if they didn't. Unlike Olympia, he thought coming out as a debutante *really* mattered, for all the wrong reasons. She was sure Veronica would grumble, and Virginia would be so excited she would want to go shopping for the dress within hours.

No one was expected to find husbands at debutante balls anymore, although now and then, and extremely rarely, a serious romance would be born that night, and then turn into marriage years later. But for the most part, the girls were escorted by cousins and brothers, or boys they had gone to school with. Asking a boyfriend to escort one seven months in advance was recognized as an invitation to trouble. At that age, on the eve of leaving for college, romances, no matter how hot and heavy they had been in June, usually didn't last till December. All the evening was solid, reliable, intelligent men who treated them well. Preferably, a man like Harry, and not their father. Now, more than anything, coming out was just an excuse to look lovely, and wear long white gloves and a beautiful white evening gown, often the first one the girls presented had ever worn. It was going to be fun helping Veronica and Virginia pick their dresses, particularly as she knew the choices the girls would make would be so different, as they always were. Having twins come out at The Arches was going to be double the fun for her. She sat staring dreamily at the invitation, with a gentle smile of memory and nostalgia on her face, as Max watched. He didn't often see his mom look like that. She felt almost like a young girl again, as memories of her own coming out flooded back to her, and Max observed her with interest. He could see that she was thinking of something that made her happy.

"What's that, Mom?" Max asked, wiping the grape juice off his chin with the back of his hand, and then brushing his hand against his jeans instead of his napkin.

"It's an invitation for your sisters," she said, slipping it back into the envelope, as she reminded herself to ask the committee for a duplicate invitation, so she could start an album for each girl, just like the one she had of her own debut, tucked away in the far as Max was concerned, birthday parties were more fun. "Do I have to go?"

"Nope. Just the grown-ups." In fact, upholding the traditions of the event, no one younger than the correct age to be presented could come. Younger siblings were never allowed to attend. She suspected that one of them would want Charlie as an escort, and had no idea who the other twin would ask. Probably one of their friends. That was up to them. Her guess was that Veronica would corral Charlie, and Ginny would ask a friend. They had four weeks to respond, but there was no need to wait. She would send the check in the following week. The fee to participate was very small, and was donated to a designated charity, which benefited from the event. It was impossible to pay one's way in. It was not about money, it was about being asked, either as a legacy, as in the case of her girls, or as a result of one's blue-blooded ancestry and connections, which was also the case for her girls, although Olympia never traded on how social her family had been. It was just a fact of life for them, and something that was there, part of the furniture of their history and life. She never even thought about it. She was much prouder of her own family and accomplishments than of her family's "blue blood."

Max went upstairs to play in his room then. Harry called and said he'd be home late. He had a conference cook, and was a far more creative chef than she. His specialties were omelets and Thai food, and he was always willing to cook for the family in a pinch, particularly if she was held up at the office during the week, which was rare for her, or in a crisis with the kids, like tonight with Max sick. They had a babysitter who came in for Max on the days she was working, and she and Harry always made an effort to come straight home from the office on those days. But she shook her head. She wasn't hungry either. "Is Max okay?"

"I think so. He ran around like crazy today at soccer, and took a couple of hits in the stomach. Either that or he's got a bug. I hope the others don't get sick." They were used to it, with four kids in the house, or even three now, flu bugs spread like wildfire, even to them. They had dealt with it for years. It had been a shock to Harry at first, but he had long since gotten used to it.

As it turned out, Max was still sick the next morning, and had a mild fever, which suggested to her that it was the flu, more likely than his exertions at soccer. Olympia went out to rent videos for him, while Harry kept him company, and Max slept for most of the afternoon. The girls were out for most of the weekend, and Ginny stayed over at a friend's. They were in the ing up with interest. They were both striking-looking blue-eyed blondes. Ginny wore her long hair straight, cascading over her shoulders, and was wearing a hint of makeup. Veronica wore hers in a braid, her face was scrubbed, and she had no need to wear makeup while playing cards with her stepfather and brother, or in fact most of the time. Their looks were identical, their styles noticeably different. It always helped identify them, which Harry had found useful over the years. If they had dressed identically and worn their hair the same way, he'd have been in trouble. In fact, without clothes, hairdos, or makeup to give one clues, their mother was the only one who could always tell them apart. Even Max got confused at times, and they teased him about it.

"I said, you were both invited to come out at The Arches in December. The invitation came this week." Olympia looked pleased for both of them, as she put butter in the baked potatoes, and carved the chicken. She had already made the salad.

"You don't expect us to do that, do you?" Veronica looked up in disapproval, as Olympia nodded, and Virginia smiled from ear to ear.

"How cool, Mom! I was afraid they wouldn't ask us. Everyone at school who's doing it got their invitations earlier this week." Their father had commented do this, it's like a slap in his face." Veronica was beside herself with righteous indignation, as Virginia looked like she was about to cry.

"No one is slapping Harry's face. This is a perfectly innocuous debutante cotillion, where the two of you wear pretty white dresses, make your bow, and have a good time. And I have no idea who will be coming out with you, or what race they are. I haven't been to a deb ball in years."

"That's bullshit, Mom. You know this is a strictly WASP event, and all it's meant to do is shut people out. Nobody with a conscience should participate, and I'm not going to. I don't care what you say, or what Ginny does, I'm not going." Veronica was fighting mad as Virginia burst into tears.

"Calm down," Olympia said quietly and firmly, slightly unnerved by Veronica's extreme reaction, as Harry watched them all with a puzzled look on his face.

"May I ask what we're all talking about? From what I can gather, the girls have been invited to a meeting sponsored by the Grand Wizard of the Ku Klux Klan, and Veronica wishes to decline."

"Exactly," Veronica said, pacing around the room and fuming, as Ginny looked at her mother in horror.

"Do you mean we can't do it?" Ginny asked with a look of panic. "Mom, don't let her spoil it...*everyone sick!*" With that, she stormed out of the kitchen, and a few seconds later, they heard her slam the door to her room, as Ginny stood in the middle of the room and sobbed.

"She always does that! You can't let her do this, Mom! She ruins *everything!*"

"She hasn't ruined everything. You're both overreacting. Why don't we let everyone cool off for a day or two, and talk about it again. She'll calm down. Just leave her alone."

"She *won't* calm down," Ginny said with a look of anguish. "She's a *Communist* and I hate her!" And with that, Ginny ran out of the room in tears. A moment later they heard the door of her room slam, too, as Harry looked across the table at his wife in amazement and total consternation.

"May I ask what's going on? What are The Arches, for God's sake, and what got into the girls?" Two of their children appeared to have gone insane. Max dug into his baked potato, and calmly shook his head.

"Mom wants them to find husbands," Max said simply, "and I don't think they want to. Maybe Ginny does, because she likes boys more than Ver does. It sounds to me like Ver doesn't want to get married. Right, Mom?"

"No...yes...no, of course not." Olympia looked flustered as she sat down and looked at both of them.

"Can anyone sign up for this event?" Harry inquired with a cautious look.

"No, you have to be invited. The girls were, because they're a legacy," she said simply.

"Does it exclude people of other races and religions?" Harry then asked her pointedly. This time Olympia hesitated slightly before she answered, as Max managed to eat his baked potato and watch them with interest at the same time. He was dripping butter all over his shirt with total unconcern.

"Probably. It used to. I don't know what their policies are these days."

"Judging by Veronica's reaction, she seems to know more than you do. If what she says is true, and black, Asian, and Hispanic girls can't do it, then I agree with her. And I assume Jewish girls would be on their hit list, too."

"Oh for God's sake, Harry. Yes, it's a fancy social thing. People have been doing it for years. It's old-fashioned, it's traditional, it's Waspy, so is the Social Register, so are clubs, for heaven's sake. What about clubs that don't admit women?"

"I don't belong to a single one of them," he said succinctly. "I'm a judge on the court of appeals, I can't afford to ally myself with any discriminatory organization, and apparently this one is. You know how I feel about things like that. Do you think they would

"If that were true, clubs wouldn't exist. Private schools wouldn't exist. Okay, call it a club for WASPs, where their daughters make their debut. I just don't see why this has to be a political issue. Why can't this just be a fun night for the girls and let it go at that?"

"My mother is a Holocaust survivor," he said ominously. "You know that. And so was my father. Their entire families were wiped out by people who hated Jews. The people who run this party are racists, from what I can gather. That runs counter to everything I stand for and believe in. I want nothing to do with an event like this." He spoke to her as though she had just painted a swastika on their kitchen wall. He almost recoiled as he spoke to her, and their son watched, looking suddenly upset.

"Harry, please, don't make a big deal out of this. It's a coming-out party, that's all it is."

"Veronica is right," he said quietly, and then stood up. He hadn't touched a mouthful of his dinner. Olympia hadn't cut Max's meat, so he was working on his second baked potato. He was hungry. And the grown-ups were confusing. "I don't think the girls should participate in this party," Harry said firmly, "whether you did it or not. I'm casting my vote with Veronica. And whatever you decide to do about it, don't for a single second expect me to attend." With that, he threw his napkin on the table and walked out said, smiling ruefully. "We don't want husbands for them, sweetheart. All we want are a couple of white dresses, and some boys to dance with them."

"I don't think Dad will go," Max said, shaking his head, as his mother cut his meat. They were the only two at the table, and Olympia had no desire to eat. She knew the girls' father would have a fit if they didn't make their debut. Politically, he was at the opposite end of the spectrum from Harry. Her old life and her new, as typified by both husbands, had absolutely nothing in common. She was the bridge between the two.

"I hope Daddy will go," Olympia said quietly to her son. "It's a fun thing to do."

"It doesn't sound like fun to me," Max said, shaking his head solemnly. "I don't think Ginny and Ver should come out," he said, looking up at his mother with wide eyes. "I think they better stay in." Given everyone's reactions that night, it was beginning to sound like it to her, too.

jections to the event, he sided with Virginia and Olympia, and said he thought both girls should come out. All their cousins in Newport had, and he knew, as Olympia did, that their father would be upset if they didn't. Harry would be upset if they did. One way or the other, everyone was going to be unhappy about something. Olympia and Harry hadn't even been speaking to each other when they both left for work, which was a rare occurrence for them. They hardly ever fought. But this time, the battle lines had been drawn.

Predictably, as always, Chauncey did not make things better, but worse.

"What kind of rabble-rousing left-wing household are you running there, Olympia, if Veronica thinks that making her debut is a persecution of the Great Unwashed? You all sound like a bunch of Commies to me." It was just the kind of thing Olympia expected him to say.

"Oh for God's sake, Chauncey, they're kids. They get emotional. Veronica has always had extreme political ideas; she's the champion of the underdog. She thinks she's a combination of Mother Teresa and Che Guevara. She'll outgrow it. This is her way of expressing herself. Seven months from now, I think she'll calm down and do it, if we don't make too big a deal of it now. If we do, she'll dig her heels in. So let's

Harry's better, but he was being silly too. "She has a strong social conscience. We just have to let her calm down, and hopefully when she does, she'll see that no one is being hurt by this. It's just a fun evening, and something nice for them to do. Don't get in an argument with her, and if you threaten her about tuition, she's liable to do something ridiculous and decide not to go to school."

"This is what you get for marrying a radical Jew." His words rang out like shots, as she sat immobilized in her seat. She couldn't believe he had the nerve to say something like that. She wanted to strangle him.

"What did you just say?" she said in an icy tone.

"You heard what I said," he fired back at her in clipped, aristocratic tones. He sounded so snobby sometimes that he sounded like a 1930s movie. No one spoke that way anymore, at any level of society, only Chauncey and Felicia did, and a handful of snobs like them.

"Don't you *ever* say something like that to me again. You're not fit to wipe his feet. It's no wonder Veronica is off the deep end over this, with an example like you. My God, have you ever bothered to notice that there's a whole world of people out there, not just idiots like you, with polo ponies?" He hadn't had a real job in twenty years. First he had lived off his grandmother, then his inheritance, and she suspected matory, he would seize it every time. And Felicia was even dumber than he. Olympia could no longer even remotely imagine how she had ever married him, even at twenty-two. At forty-four, she would rather have cut her head off than be married to him for ten minutes. Just talking to him drove her insane.

"I don't want you threatening Veronica about her tuition. If you do that, she'll do something even more stupid. Let's keep this about the party, and not about tuition or school. You can't do that to the girls. I can take you to court over it if I have to." He had an obligation to pay the girls' tuition, although she knew he was foolish enough not to pay it just to prove a point, despite the consequences to him.

"Go ahead, take me to court, Olympia. I don't give a damn if you do. If you don't give Veronica my message, I will. In fact, just to make sure she doesn't do something stupid, you can tell her I won't pay tuition for either of them, unless they both come out next Christmas. Veronica won't want to screw it up for Ginny, and if Veronica doesn't agree to come out, she will. I don't care if you put me in jail. I'm not paying a red cent for either of them, unless they both make their debut. Put Veronica in handcuffs, or sedate her if you have to, but she *will* come out at The Arches!" He was every bit as stubborn as his daughter, and more so. He was turning this into a major war for all now he was doing it again, over a debutante party. It was beginning to sound crazy to her, too.

"I'm not going to have a daughter who won't come out. For heaven's sake, Olympia, think of the embarrassment that will cause."

"I can think of worse things," Olympia said glumly. But Chauncey couldn't, obviously. Not being a debutante was worse than death to him. Olympia wanted them to have fun, even if it seemed silly, but she wasn't willing to threaten their lives over it. If Veronica truly refused to do it, she wasn't going to force her, and Virginia could still come out, with or without her twin. Chauncey's ploy of holding her hostage was just too extreme, and too unfair, to all of them, her too.

"I can't think of anything more humiliating, and I'm not going to be pushed around by her. You can tell her I said so, Olympia."

"Why don't you tell her yourself?" Olympia said, tired of being in the middle. It was just going to make Veronica madder at her. If he wanted to threaten her to that degree, let him do it himself.

"I will," he said, sounding furious. "I don't know how you've brought up these girls. At least Ginny has some sense."

"I think we need to let this cool down," Olympia said sensibly. "We can deal with it in September, or

"Do you want Felicia to talk to her?" Olympia nearly groaned at the suggestion. Felicia was not known for her tact, nor her popularity with either girl. They tolerated her for their father's sake, but thought her irritating and stupid. Olympia agreed.

"I'll deal with it myself." She managed to get off the phone with him before she lost her temper, which was a minor miracle. Everything about Chauncey Walker made her want to strangle him. She was still furious about their conversation, when her mother-in-law called her that afternoon. Olympia was up to her ears in work, preparing a case for litigation, when her secretary told her that Mrs. Rubinstein was on the phone. Olympia had no idea what it was about. She just hoped it wasn't the ball. Harry whining to his mother was unlike him, but anything seemed possible now. The whole family was up in arms, from Newport to New York.

"Hi, Frieda," Olympia said, sounding tired. She was stressed about the family issues, and had had a long day at work. "Everything all right?"

"You tell me. Veronica called and said she was mad at you, and wants to spend the night." Olympia pursed her lips. She didn't like the idea of Veronica trying to run away from irritants at home, although she valued the close relationship both girls had with Harry's mother. She was a kind, warm, wise woman

47

nuts over them, or boycotting them. All clubs had the right to let in who they wanted, and she thought this would be a wonderful experience for the girls. She thought Veronica should do it, and intended to tell her so, if she had the chance. Harry told her she was far too liberal for his taste, and left her apartment in a huff after lunch. He was still upset when he went back to his office. Olympia hadn't heard from him all day. "I'm sorry Veronica bothered you with this," Olympia apologized. "It's a tempest in a teapot, but for the moment, everyone's getting burned, and very steamed up."

"How can I help?" Frieda said practically. She was a wonderful, intelligent woman, with a youthful outlook for her age, and an incredibly forgiving nature, given the childhood experiences she'd had. She rarely if ever talked about it, but Olympia knew from Harry how terrifying and devastating it was for her, losing her entire family, and living through the torture in the camps. She had had nightmares for years, and had very wisely undergone therapy. Her attitude was extraordinary, and Olympia had nothing but the profoundest affection and respect for her. She felt blessed to be related to her.

"I don't think you can help, Frieda. They'll all settle down. It's a long, silly story. The girls were invited to make their debut at the ball where I came out years

"Tell them all to take a hike," the older woman said sanely. "Go shopping for a dress with Ginny, and buy one for Veronica. Tell my son to get over himself. The Nazis are setting fire to synagogues in Germany, they don't have time for white-tie events, or even black-tie ones." She had said exactly that to him herself. "Don't pay any attention to them. Veronica needs to let off steam. She'll do it in the end. What are you going to wear?" Frieda asked with a tone of interest, and Olympia laughed. It was the most sensible question she could have asked.

"A straitjacket if they don't all calm down." And then she thought of something, and wondered how her mother-in-law would react, given what Harry had said. "Frieda, would you like to come?"

"Are you serious?" She sounded stunned. From what Harry had said, she had assumed that wouldn't be possible, if the event was in fact anti-Semitic, and she would never have asked to come, nor expected it. Even operating under that assumption, she still thought the twins should come out, whether or not she was there. She was extremely generous about never forcing herself on her daughter-in-law, her son, or their children. She was incredibly discreet, and had been wonderful to Olympia from the first, unlike her first mother-in-law, who had been a beast, and the

Harry in the opposite sense. It represented everything she had been excluded from and cheated of as a
young girl, and was a form of victory and validation
for her. There had been no balls or parties in her
youth. There had been poverty and hard work in
sweatshops. Knowing that her daughter-in-law
wanted her at an event like that meant the world to
her, and Olympia wouldn't have deprived her of it
for anything on earth. Olympia could hear in Frieda's
voice how much it meant to her.

"I have to find something with long sleeves," she
said softly, and Olympia understood. She wanted to
cover her tattoo, as she always did.

"We'll find the perfect dress. I promise," Olympia
said gently.

"Good. I'll work on Veronica this weekend. She
shouldn't spoil it for her sister. Cesar Chavez will
never know she went, and it'll be more fun for both of
them if they both go. And tell my son not to be such a
pain in the neck. He just doesn't want to wear a tux.
And if he won't go, we'll have a good time without
him. December is a long way off, they'll all calm
down by then. Don't let them upset you," Frieda said
in a loving tone, which was typical of all of Olympia's
dealings with her in the thirteen years of her marriage to Harry. Olympia had won her mother-in-law's
love and loyalty forever when she converted to

graduate, and then on to Yale Law School. She happened to be African American and Olympia wasn't anxious to explain her problems to her, but after circling the subject cautiously for five minutes, she finally spelled it out to her. Margaret had exactly the same reaction Olympia's mother-in-law had had. "Oh for chrissake, we poison the environment, we sell cigarettes and alcohol, half the nation's youth is hooked on drugs they can buy on street corners, not to mention guns, we have one of the highest suicide rates in the world among youth under the age of twenty-five, we get into wars that are none of our goddamn business at every opportunity, Social Security is bankrupt or damn near it, the nation is crippled by debt. Our politicians are crooked for the most part, our educational system is falling apart, and you're supposed to feel guilty about your kids playing Cinderella for one night at some fancy Waspy ball? Give me a break. I've got news for you, there are no whites at my mother's bingo club in Harlem either, and she doesn't feel guilty for a goddamn minute. Harry knows better— why don't you tell him to go picket someone? This isn't a Nazi youth movement, it's a bunch of silly girls in pretty white dresses. Hell, if I were in your shoes, and I had a kid, I'd want her to do it, too. And I wouldn't feel guilty about it, either. Tell everyone to relax. It doesn't bother me, and I boycotted just about more, it's about wearing a dress and going to a party. That's all it is. A one-night stand for tradition and the family album. Not a travesty of social values."

"Believe me, I never lost a night's sleep over it when I was a kid, and I knew girls at Harvard who did it in New York and Boston. In fact, one of them invited me to go, but I was modeling in Chicago that weekend to pay for school."

"I hope you come," Olympia said generously, and Margaret grinned.

"I'd love to." It never even remotely occurred to Olympia that Margaret being there would cause a stir, nor did she care. So far, she had invited a Jewish woman as her guest, and an African American, and she was Jewish now herself. And if the committee didn't like it for some reason, though she doubted it, she didn't give a damn.

"I just hope Harry comes, too," she said, looking sad. She hated fighting with him.

"If he doesn't, it's his loss, and he'll look stupid. Give him time to come down off his high horse. It should tell him something that his mother approves and thinks the girls should do it."

"Yeah," Olympia said with a sigh. "Now all I have to do is convince the girls. Or Veronica at least. If not, she and Harry can picket the event. Maybe they can carry signs objecting to the women wearing fur."

to work it out before December. His only comment to her was late one night after Charlie came home from Dartmouth for the weekend and mentioned it. Harry said only three words to both of them, which said it all.

"I'm not going," he growled, and then left the room, leaving Olympia to discuss it with her elder son.

"That's fine," Olympia said quietly, remembering what his mother had said, and Margaret Washington. She had seven months to change his mind.

Charlie agreed to be Ginny's escort for the ball, although she had recently met a boy she liked. She had taken her mother's advice about not inviting a romantic interest to be her escort for the ball. A lot could change in seven months. Olympia was counting on it. She still needed to turn Harry and Veronica around. For the moment at least, everyone seemed to have calmed down.

nis one Saturday morning, while Charlie babysat for Max. She and Harry loved playing tennis and squash with each other. It gave them time alone and relaxed them both. They cherished the time they managed to spend alone, which was infrequent, as they spent most of their evenings and weekend time with Max. With Charlie home, they had a built-in babysitter. He was always quick to volunteer to take care of Max for them.

"I haven't noticed anything," Harry said, wiping his face with a towel, after the game. He had beaten her, but barely. They had both played a good game, and were in great shape. She had just shared her concerns about Charlie with him, and he was surprised to hear that Olympia thought Charlie was out of sorts. "He seems fine to me."

"He doesn't to me. He hasn't said anything, but whenever he doesn't know I'm watching him, he looks depressed, or pensive, or just sad somehow. Or worried. I don't know what it is. Maybe he's unhappy at school."

"You worry too much, Ollie," he said, smiling at her, and then he leaned over and kissed her. "That was a good game. I had fun."

"Yeah." She grinned at him as he put an arm around her. "Because you won. You always say it was a good game when you win."

him gently then, and he kissed her. She always had a good time with him. And she was pleased to see that he'd relaxed finally, after their battles about the ball. He still said he wasn't coming, but she hadn't mentioned it to him in a while. She wanted to let the subject cool off before she tried again.

They talked about Charlie again as they walked home. "I just have the feeling something is bothering him, but he doesn't seem to want to talk."

"If you're right, he'll talk to you eventually," Harry reassured her. "He always does." He knew how close Olympia was to her older son, just as she was to the twins, and to Max. She was a terrific mother, and a wonderful wife. There was so much he admired about her and always had. Just as she loved and respected him. And he knew she had great instincts for her kids. If she thought something was upsetting Charlie, maybe she was right, although she felt more relaxed about it after discussing it with Harry. "Maybe he got his heart broken over some girl." They both wondered if it was that. Charlie hadn't had a serious romance in a while. He went out a lot, and played the field. He hadn't had a serious girl in his life in nearly two years.

"I don't think it's that. I think he'd tell me if it was about a girl. It seems deeper than that to me. He just looks sad."

the deep end. Charlie seemed fine to him. They played golf together over several weekends, and Charlie came down to have lunch at his office. He said he was thinking of going to divinity school after he graduated, and the ministry appealed to him. Harry was impressed by what he said, and the insights he had about people and delicate situations. Charlie broached the deb ball with him once or twice, and Harry refused to discuss it with him. He said that he disapproved of an event that excluded anyone, tacitly or otherwise, and he had taken a stand.

So had Veronica, but her position seemed to be softening by the time the girls left for Europe in July with their friends. Ginny had ordered a dress by then, a beautiful white taffeta strapless ballgown with tiny pearls sewn in a flower pattern in a wide border along the hem. It looked like a wedding gown, and Ginny was thrilled with it. And without saying anything to Veronica, Ginny and her mother had chosen a narrow white satin column with a diagonal band across one shoulder that looked like something Veronica would wear. It was sexy, sleek, and backless and would show off her slim figure. Ginny preferred her big ballgown. Both dresses were exquisite, and although the girls were identical, the dresses would set off the differences between them, and underline their contrasting styles. Olympia had hidden the satin dress in her

After that, they went to the Riviera. They spent a few days in St. Tropez, a night in Monte Carlo, and a few days in Cannes. Max played on the beach, and started picking up a few words of French from a group of children his own age. At the end of a week, all three of them were rested, happy, and tanned. They had spent the whole week eating bouillabaisse, lobster, and fish. Max sent Charlie a T-shirt from St. Tropez, and Charlie sent them a steady stream of funny postcards, reporting on his adventures in camp. He seemed to be having a great time.

They were once again sad to leave, when Olympia, Harry, and Max flew from Nice to Venice to meet the girls. And all five of them had a terrific time in Venice. They visited every church and monument. Max fed the pigeons in the Piazza San Marco, and they all took a gondola ride under the Bridge of Sighs. Harry kissed Olympia as they passed under it, which the gondolier said meant they would belong to each other forever. As they kissed, Max scrunched his face up and the twins smiled at them and laughed at Max.

Their subsequent trip through northern Italy and into Switzerland was an unforgettable family time. They stayed at a beautiful hotel on Lake Geneva, traveled through the Alps, and wound up in London for the last few days. Max said he had loved all of it, and they all admitted that they were sad the twins home from Europe. "It's just not right. Why should Mom be punished because you won't do it?" Ginny had finally gotten under her skin, as had Harry's mother, who quietly took Veronica to lunch before they left, and asked her to be a good sport about it. And on her last night in New York, she agreed. Veronica swore she would hate doing it, and still disapproved of it violently, but her father's unreasonable position finally did it for her. She didn't want him to penalize their mother, so she grudgingly agreed. Olympia thanked her profusely, and promised to try and make it as painless as possible for her. Veronica tried on the dress and said she hated it, but it looked spectacular on her. She didn't have an escort yet, but promised to think about it. She had to give the committee his name by Thanksgiving.

"What about one of Charlie's friends?" Olympia suggested, and Veronica said she'd come up with someone herself. It was enough for now that she had agreed to do it, she didn't want to be bugged about her escort, so Olympia backed off. The only remaining protester was Harry, who refused to even discuss the matter with her. He was disappointed that Veronica had conceded, but given her father's manipulative and punitive position, he agreed that it had been the decent thing for her to do, for her mother's sake. But there was no penalty for his not attending.

everyone he met liked him. He was thinking about a teaching job, too. He was all over the map.

"Poor kid, I'd hate to be young again," Olympia commented to Harry the day she'd had lunch with Charlie. "He's feeling pulled in about four hundred directions. His father wants him to come to Newport and train polo ponies with him. Thank God that's not one of the options he's considering." Nor was working in Chauncey's family's bank in New York. He had decided against it. Charlie wanted to do something different, he just hadn't figured out what yet. Harry thought he should go to Oxford. Olympia liked the sound of the job in San Francisco. And Charlie himself wasn't sure. Harry had also suggested law school, which Charlie had resisted. He still liked the idea of divinity school best of all. "I can't see him as a minister," Olympia said honestly, although he was religious, more so than the rest of the family.

"Maybe it would suit him," Harry said, looking pensive. "He won't make money at it. It would be nice if he had another option, something a little more profit-oriented." The job in San Francisco was actually in Palo Alto, with a computer company, which Olympia had encouraged him to seriously consider. He was planning to go out and visit his friend and his father after Christmas, after he escorted his sister to the deb ball. The whole family was planning to go to

"He's still young. He'll find his way. How is his relationship with his father these days?" She knew it had been strained off and on over the past fifteen years. Chauncey was always disappointing. He seemed to be far more interested in the three daughters he had with Felicia than the three children from his previous marriage. The twins didn't seem bothered by it, but Charlie always felt let down by him. Harry did his best to be supportive of him, but Charlie's own father's seeming indifference to him weighed heavily on him. It was just the way Chauncey was. Superficial, with a short attention span, and a strong dislike for responsibility. If it wasn't fun, and couldn't be done on horseback, he didn't do it. He had always wanted Charlie to play polo, and was annoyed he hadn't. Charlie had told Frieda on several occasions that he thought it was a stupid game.

"His relationship with Chauncey is nonexistent," Olympia said, looking troubled. "And Harry is so busy, he doesn't have a lot of time to spend with him. Charlie doesn't open up a lot with anyone these days." She told her then of his friend's suicide the previous spring. "He didn't say much about it, but I got a bill for counseling from Dartmouth, and he said that's why he went. He was still upset when he came home in June. But he was his old self in August when he came back from Colorado."

both another cup of tea. They had had a lovely afternoon together, as they always did.

"Maybe he should be a rabbi, instead of a minister. My father was a wonderful rabbi, he was so kind with people, and such a wise, learned man." It was rare that she spoke of her parents, and it always touched Olympia when she did.

"Chauncey would be thrilled." They both laughed at the thought of her snobbish ex-husband's reaction to Charlie converting and becoming a rabbi. "I love the idea. It would drive him insane."

Frieda had only met Chauncey and Felicia once, and he had been barely civil to her. She wasn't even a blip on his radar screen. He had instantly dismissed her, as he did anyone who was not part of his familiar social world. Olympia knew he would be annoyed that she had invited Frieda to The Arches. More than likely, he would ignore her, and he would be even more upset that she had invited Margaret Washington to join them as well. Elderly Jewish women and African Americans were not Chauncey's idea of appropriate guests for a debutante cotillion. It was easy for Olympia to imagine the kind of guests they would bring, if they did. All very Social Register, snobbishly aristocratic, and boring as dirt. At least Frieda was fun and interesting to talk to, she had traveled widely, read constantly, loved to talk politics, and had a warm

"He's still not going," Max said with a serious expression.

"I know." Olympia smiled at her youngest son.

"You're not mad at him anymore?" Max was concerned.

"No. He has a right to his opinions." As she said it, Harry walked back in, and she spoke directly to him. "Although your position about not going to the ball is actually discriminatory. You're discriminating against WASPs."

"They're discriminating against blacks and Jews."

"I guess you're even then," she said calmly. "I'm not sure one discrimination is better than the other. It seems about the same to me."

"You've been talking to my mother," he said, tossing the salad. "She just wants an excuse to get dressed up. You all do. You're losing sight of what this kind of thing means."

"It's just a rite of passage, Harry. There's no malice behind it, and the girls will be disappointed if you don't go. That seems worse to me, hurting people you love and who love you, in order to make a statement to people you don't know, and who won't care that you're not there. We will."

"You'll be fine without me. Max and I will stay here."

"What are they going to come out of?" Max asked,

then give her his arm, and they'll walk down the stairs. And afterward, the girls will dance with their dad."

"Both of them at the same time?" It sounded complicated to Max.

"No, one at a time." The other twin could have danced with Harry, if he'd been there, and then switched. This way, without him, they would have to take turns.

"Who's going to walk Veronica down the stairs?"

"We don't know yet. Veronica has to figure it out by Thanksgiving."

"He better be good, so he can catch her if she falls over while she does that thing you just did, or if she falls down the stairs." Harry and Olympia both laughed and their eyes met, as he put their steaks on plates. And then suddenly Olympia laughed at the memory of her own escort. She hadn't thought of it in years.

"My date got drunk before we got out onstage. He passed out, and they had to find another boy to go onstage with me. I'd never met him before, but he was very nice."

"I bet they got really mad at the one who got drunk."

"Yes, they did." She remembered, too, and didn't mention, that it had been the last time she danced with her father. He had died the following year, and later she had cherished the bittersweet memory of hood, and your entry into an adult world. Watching Veronica and Virginia go through it was something she would have liked to share with him.

Harry still didn't see it that way. He thought it was more important to make a statement about the political incorrectness of the event. Max asked a number of questions about bar mitzvahs then, and Harry talked about his. It was a time he would always remember with tenderness and joy. Max was already excited thinking about his, and it was seven years away.

The girls called as Olympia and Harry were cleaning up after dinner. They liked their classes, and said everything was fine at school. They were sharing a suite with each other and two other girls. Charlie had a single room that year, as a lofty senior at Dartmouth. He had opted to live on campus, in the dorms. He had talked about getting a house with a bunch of roommates, and decided against it in the end. He said he didn't mind living in the dorms again. They hadn't heard from him since the day he left. They knew he was busy, and had a lot to do as he started his senior year. None of the older children was coming home before Thanksgiving. It felt like too long to Olympia before she saw them again. It made her more grateful than ever that they had Max, and another twelve years to look forward to with him.

Harry and Olympia put Max to bed together that

# Chapter 4

*All of the children* came home for Thanksgiving. Charlie came home on Tuesday, the girls on Wednesday. They had just gone through the agony of midterms, and all three of the older children felt liberated and free. Max was thrilled to have them too, and loved playing with them. Charlie picked him up at school the day he got home, and took him to Central Park, to the zoo. He bought him hot chestnuts and a balloon. And the following afternoon, he took him skating. They returned with pink cheeks, bright eyes, and in great spirits. By the time they got home, the girls had arrived, and they shared a lively dinner before Charlie and the twins went out afterward to meet their friends. Their noisy presence in the house reminded Olympia of how much she loved having all of her children at home.

"Well enough," Veronica said casually. "I've been going out with him for about three weeks."

"What happens if you stop dating him before the cotillion? That could be awkward." Everyone always agreed that boyfriends made bad escorts, because if you stopped seeing them just before the ball, you could wind up without a date.

"He's just a friend," Veronica said, looking unconcerned. She had agreed to make her debut, but without any enthusiasm. She was only doing it so her father wouldn't withdraw his share of the tuition for school. But she was still angry about his blackmail and manipulation. She had told everyone repeatedly that she fully anticipated having a rotten time at the ball. She was the original reluctant debutante, but Ginny more than made up for what her twin sister lacked in excitement about the event. She couldn't wait, and had tried on her dress four times in the last two days. It was the ballgown of her dreams. Charlie had checked the night he got back, and said his tuxedo still fit, although he said it was a little tight in the waist, but nothing he couldn't live with for one night.

Veronica had said that her escort wanted to meet Charlie and Ginny, but he had gone skiing in Vermont over the Thanksgiving weekend.

"What's he like?" Charlie asked with interest. It

smiled from ear to ear. She had been able to think of nothing else for the past many weeks.

Harry's mother stayed until nearly midnight. He put her in a cab and sent her home, and as he went out to help her, he saw that it was snowing.

By morning, the city was blanketed by snow. After lunch they all agreed to go to Central Park, and when they did, they wrapped garbage bags around their bottoms, and slid down the hills. Max rapidly became an expert at it, and Harry wasn't bad at it, either. It was a lot of fun, and Olympia laughed with pleasure as she slid down the hills. The girls lay in the snow, and made angels by waving their arms as far up and down as they could, making impressions that looked like wings in the fresh snow. They had been doing that since they were little children, and loved it more than ever. Afterward, they all went to Rockefeller Center, skated, and had dinner. After they got back to the house, they called their friends, figured out plans, and the three oldest ones went out shortly after to meet up with people, or hang out in their homes. Max was sound asleep by the time they left, exhausted after a long, busy day. He had worn himself out making a snowman with his older brother.

"It's been a wonderful Thanksgiving," Olympia said to Harry as they got into bed and slid under the sheets. "It's so nice to have the kids home. I miss needed to spill the beans. She was madly in love with a junior at Brown she said. He was the coolest boy she'd ever met. Like the boy Veronica was dating and bringing to the ball, he was on the football team. His name was Steve, and Ginny was head over heels in love with him, unlike Veronica, who liked her date, but for the moment was nothing more than friends with him. Ginny told her mother she had been seeing him three or four times a week for three months. And she asked if he could come to the ball, too. Olympia had reserved a table, and said she would save a seat for him. Ginny was thrilled. Since her brother was her official escort, there was no conflict in having Steve there, too. She said he was from Boston, from a very respectable family. He was a twin, too, and his brother was at Duke. From everything she said to Olympia, he sounded like a nice kid.

Olympia told Harry about it that afternoon, and said she was pleased for her, although she hoped Ginny's studies wouldn't suffer from the amount of time she was spending with him. Ginny had said they studied together, and spent a lot of time in the library when he wasn't at practice with the team. "She's so crazy about him, it's really cute."

Olympia looked delighted. Ginny had had a number of crushes in high school, and several boyfriends. Her romances usually lasted a few months. Veronica

Ginny were looking for a younger version of her elusive, inattentive father. And it sounded as though she was head over heels in love with Steve.

Virginia had admitted to her mother that they were sleeping together, but had promised her that they always used protection. But the degree of her infatuation with him worried her mother anyway, particularly after what Veronica said.

"I get the feeling you don't like him," Olympia said honestly, fishing for more reasons why, if not.

"He's okay. I'm not crazy about him. Someone told me he jerks girls around a lot. I don't want her to get hurt," Veronica said honestly, with worried eyes. But once Ginny got an idea in her head, she was hard to stop. About anything. Veronica was stubborn, too, though usually about ideas, not people.

"I don't want her to get hurt either," Olympia said. Ginny was obviously moving full steam ahead. "Keep an eye on her, please. Talk sense to her, if you need to," Olympia said conspiratorially, as Veronica laughed and rolled her eyes.

"Yeah. Sure. A lot of good that would do me with Ginny. You know how she is." Mostly, with Ginny, all you could do was help her pick up the pieces later. When she fell, she fell hard. And when it was over, her whole world came crashing down around her. In he'd do it." He had also said they could get stoned before they went on stage for her to make her bow. But she didn't share that piece of information with her mother. She thought it was funny, whether they did it or not.

"Does he look normal?" Olympia asked with some trepidation, as Veronica gave her a dark look, with obvious irritation.

"No, Mom, he has three heads, and a bone through his nose. Yeah, he looks normal, most of the time. He knows the drill. He'll look fine that night."

"What does he look like the rest of the time?" Olympia asked gingerly.

"Sort of punk, but nothing too outrageous. He spikes his hair, but he said he didn't for his sister's debut. He'll be fine, Mom. Don't worry."

"I hope so," Olympia said with a sigh. She was beginning to feel stressed about the event, and she wouldn't have Harry to lean on. She, Frieda, Margaret Washington and her husband, another couple, Ginny's new boyfriend Steve, and Chauncey and Felicia would be sharing a table. A motley crew at best. The debutantes and their escorts would be seated elsewhere.

Olympia mentioned her concerns to Charlie before he went back to school, and he assured his mother everything would be all right. It was only one evening. Nothing much was going to happen. The girls would had decided not to go after Christmas, and to go over spring break instead. He had also applied to Oxford for a year of graduate studies, before applying to divinity school at Harvard. He had options and choices, and decisions to make, which was stressful for him. He had his whole life ahead of him to work out. It was always important to Charlie to feel he was doing the right thing.

"Don't worry too much about what you're going to do. You'll figure it out. The right thing will just happen. Give it time."

"I know it will be okay, Mom." He leaned over and kissed her. "Don't you worry, either. Have you talked to Dad lately?"

She shook her head. "Not since last summer, when he was so mad at Veronica saying she wouldn't come out."

"Maybe you should just call him to say hi, so it's not too awkward that night." He knew how much his mother disliked Felicia, and how strained her relationship had become with Chauncey. They had absolutely nothing in common.

It was a mystery to all the children how their parents had ever gotten married. Seven years together was remarkable between people who were that mismatched, although at twenty-two Olympia had been a different person. She had been a product of her own very conservative Episcopalian upbringing, and be flattered by the call. Chauncey liked homage and attention.

"Maybe I will call him," Olympia said cautiously. She wasn't enthused about it, but recognized it as a diplomatic suggestion. "Are you going up to see him over Christmas break?"

"I thought I'd go up for a couple of days, before we go to Aspen." Harry, Olympia, and all the children were going to Colorado over Christmas for a week of skiing, as they did every year. They all looked forward to it. Charlie never admitted it to anyone, but it was more fun being with them than with his father. But he went to see him out of loyalty and affection, and always the hope that they would be able to connect somehow, at a deeper level. So far that had never happened. Chauncey wasn't a deep person. "He has some new polo ponies he wants to show me." Charlie looked sad as he said it. He knew what a disappointment it was to his father that he didn't want to play polo. He liked riding with him, and had ridden to hounds with him in Europe, just to see what it was like, but polo bored him. It was his father's passion.

"Do you want to bring any friends with you to Aspen?" They rented a house there, and Olympia was always open to the kids bringing friends with them. It was more fun for them if they did, but Charlie shook his head, after a flicker of hesitation.

night. When they came home in December, there wouldn't be time to alter it before the rehearsal and ball.

"You both have shoes, right?" Ginny had bought hers in July, perfectly plain white satin pumps, with little pearls on them, just like her dress. They had been lucky to find them. Veronica insisted she had a pair of white satin evening sandals in her closet.

"You're sure?" Olympia asked again. They both had evening bags, long white kid gloves, and the string of pearls with matching earrings she had bought each of them for their eighteenth birthdays. That was all they needed.

"I'm sure," Veronica said, rolling her eyes. "Do you realize how much more worthwhile it would be if we spent the money on people who are starving in Appalachia?"

"The two are not mutually exclusive. Harry and I give plenty of money to charity, Veronica. He does more pro bono work than anyone I know, and I do my share. You don't need to feel guilty over one dress and a pair of sandals."

"I'd rather spend the night working in a homeless shelter."

"That's noble of you. You can atone for your sins when we get back from Aspen." They had a month's vacation, and she was sure that Veronica would be dren. She was complaining about their school in Newport, and how stupid it was that they had to wear uniforms, instead of the cute little outfits she bought them in Boston and New York. She was nice enough to say though that she was looking forward to the girls' debut at The Arches, and Olympia thanked her and asked for Chauncey. Felicia said he had just come in for lunch, from the stables. It still amazed Olympia that her ex-husband had been content not to work for the past fifteen years, and live off his family fortune. She couldn't imagine a life like that, even if she could afford it. She loved her law practice, and respected Harry for all he had accomplished. In his entire lifetime, Chauncey had achieved nothing. All he did was play polo, and buy horses. In their early days together, he had worked in his family's bank, but he had given that up quickly. It took too much effort, and was too much trouble. Now he made no pretense about the indolent life he led, and always jokingly said that work was for the masses. He was a snob to his core.

He sounded out of breath when he came on the line. He had run up from the stables, and was surprised when Felicia told him Olympia was calling. Unless something dire was happening, she never called him. Whatever plans or information she needed to share, she sent by e-mail.

girls had been impressed by his Ferrari when they last saw him.

"That should be nice," Olympia said benignly. "Will you be here for long?" She wondered if she should invite them to the house for drinks, but cringed at the prospect, and she knew Harry would, too. The two men grudgingly acknowledged each other. Harry was polite to him, but Chauncey was barely civil. He ignored him.

"Just the weekend. Is Veronica behaving?" Chauncey asked with interest.

"Seems like it. She finally lined up an escort. Some boy called Jeff Adams. She swears he's respectable. I hope she's right."

"If he's not, or looks like hell, the committee will kick him out at the rehearsal. Any idea who his parents are?" He didn't ask if Jeff's parents were in the Social Register, but Olympia knew he'd like to.

"None. All she said is that his sister came out last year," which meant that he would pass muster for Chauncey. That was all it took. The criteria were simple for him.

"Ask her what his father's name is. I can look them up in the Social Register, maybe I know them." For once, it might be reassuring. The Social Register ran Chauncey's life, the way some people's were ruled by the Bible. It was his Bible. Olympia didn't even own would never have said that to either wife. "Is your husband coming?" He had no idea why he had asked her that, it seemed obvious that he would, and Chauncey was surprised when she hesitated.

"No, actually. He isn't. He has some family event he has to go to," and then she remembered that Frieda would be there, and decided to be honest with him. "Actually, that's not true. He thinks the whole idea is politically incorrect, and excludes people of other races and colors, so he's not coming."

"That's too bad for you," he said, sounding sympathetic for once. "Felicia and I will look out for you." It was the nicest he had been in years, and Olympia was glad that she had followed Charlie's suggestion. It warmed things up a bit and broke the ice before the inevitable stresses and tensions of the big night. The girls would be nervous wrecks, and she suspected she would be, too, getting them ready, getting them there, and making sure that all was right. Not to mention an escort for Veronica whom she'd never met, and her attitude about the event. Olympia realized it was still possible, right up to the last second, for Veronica to back out. She just hoped she wouldn't, and had already told Harry several times not to stir her up, or encourage her to do anything foolish. He had promised he wouldn't.

"Anything I can do for you before you come?"

"Me too." Olympia smiled, grateful for her friend's support. It was more than she could say for Harry. It was a shame he felt he had to make such an issue of it. The only one it hurt was her.

"Has Harry backed down yet?" Margaret asked cautiously, setting the briefs down on Olympia's desk. She wanted her opinion on them.

"No. I don't think he will. We all worked on him about it. I've finally given up. At least for once Chauncey isn't being a horse's ass. Although God knows how he'll be that night." He tended to drink a lot, although less than when he'd been married to her, according to friends. In his youth, he had been drunk for most of their marriage. In the early days, it made him charming and amorous. Later, he turned surly and nasty. It was impossible to predict how he'd behave with four martinis and a bottle of wine in him on the night of the ball, or worse yet, once he got into the brandy. But for the moment at least, he was being civil, and it was Felicia's problem now to control him once he got drunk. No longer hers, thank God. Felicia drank a lot, too. They had that in common. Olympia had never been much of a drinker, nor was Harry.

"Don't worry, Ollie. I'll be there to hold your hand," Margaret reassured her.

"I'll need it," Olympia said, as she pulled the briefs toward her, across her desk, and Margaret sat down to

# Chapter 5

*The weekend before* the coming-out ball, Olympia woke up with a raging fever. She'd been feeling funny for two days. She had a scratchy throat, a stomachache, a stuffy nose, and by Saturday night, she felt like death. Her fever was 102. She was slightly better on Sunday, but the stomachache was worse. She was practically in tears when she came downstairs on Sunday morning. Harry was making breakfast for Max, and she noticed that her son's face was bright red. She took Max's temperature right after breakfast. His was 103, and he said his tummy itched. When she looked, she saw that he had a nasty rash. It was coming up in tiny blisters, and when she took out her trusty copy of Dr. Spock, which she had kept since Charlie was born, what Max had perfectly matched the description of chicken pox, as she suspected.

home till Friday night." She sobbed miserably. She felt awful, and didn't want to miss the ball that weekend.

"You may not have any other choice than to take makeup exams."

"What if I have a red nose?"

"That's the least of it. Go to the infirmary tomorrow, and see if they'll put you on antibiotics so you don't wind up with an infection and get really sick. That should help." She had gotten them both meningitis shots before they went off to school in September, so at least she knew it wasn't anything worse than a bad cold or at worst bronchitis, and antibiotics would keep it from turning into pneumonia. Ginny sounded just terrible. So far, Veronica hadn't caught it, but sharing a tiny room with her sister, it wasn't going to surprise Olympia if she got sick, too. "Max has chicken pox," her mother said mournfully. "Thank God all of you have had it. That's all we'd need. The poor kid feels awful, too. We're a mess," Olympia said ruefully. It was turning into a hell of a week, with invalids everywhere.

On Monday, she felt better, Max felt worse, and Ginny called to say they had given her antibiotics, so Olympia was hopeful she'd feel better by the end of the week. She'd gone to take her exams and burst into tears when she called her mother, and said she was sure that she had failed. She managed to squeeze in bone. Max was propped up in bed, watching videos, and covered in calamine lotion.

"Hi, sweetheart, how's it going?"

"Itchy," he said, looking unhappy. His fever had gone up again, but at least Olympia's hadn't. She had had a miserable, stressful day in the office. And Harry had left a message at the house that he had an emergency at work, and wouldn't be home till at least nine. She couldn't wait for Charlie to come home the next day, and at least give her a hand in cheering up Max, who looked sick, feverish, and bored. Charlie was terrific with him, and Olympia was feeling overwhelmed. It didn't help that Harry was out when she felt sick herself.

She made chicken soup for herself and Max, put a frozen pizza in the microwave for him, and blew her nose about four hundred times. She had just tucked him in for the night, turned off his light, and walked into her bedroom, longing for a hot bath, when the phone rang. It was still snowing heavily outside. It was Frieda, who apologized for calling her. She knew Max had chicken pox, and inquired how he was.

"Poor kid, he looks awful. He's covered with calamine. I didn't think that many spots could fit on one child. He even has them inside his ears, nose, and mouth."

"Poor thing. How's your cold?"

some groceries before the storm got worse. I slipped on the ice. But I'm fine now." She didn't sound it.

"What happened? Did you get hurt?"

"Nothing serious," Frieda reassured her. "I'll be fine in a few days."

"How fine? Did you see a doctor?"

There was another long pause before she answered. "I broke my ankle," she said, sounding chagrined and feeling foolish. "I fell on a patch of ice on the curb. It was such a stupid thing. I should know better."

"Oh my God, how awful. Did you go to the hospital? Why didn't you call me?"

"I know how busy you are at work. I didn't want to bother you. I called Harry, but I couldn't get through. He was in a meeting."

"He still is," Olympia said, obviously distressed over her mother-in-law's accident, and that she hadn't been there to help. "You should have called me, Frieda." She hated the thought of the older woman negotiating the emergency room alone.

"They put me in an ambulance and took me to NYU." It had been quite an adventure, and she had been there all afternoon.

"Are you in a cast?" Olympia was horrified. What had happened to Frieda was far worse than Max's chicken pox, Ginny's cough, or her cold.

leave her alone at home. She might fall and break something else. She had to stay with them. "I don't want to bother you and the children," Frieda said, and as Olympia listened, she realized they must have given her something for the pain.

"You're not a bother, and there's no reason for you to stay there. Will they let you leave tonight?"

"I think so," Frieda said vaguely.

"I'll call and ask the nurse, and call you back." Olympia took down the details of her room number, the section of the hospital she was in, and the nurses' station that was nearest to her. Although she had obviously been sedated, she was remarkably coherent, and kept apologizing for being a pain in the neck. "You're not," Olympia assured her, and hung up. She tried calling Harry at the office, but his private line was on voicemail, and his secretary had left. It was after eight o'clock.

She called the hospital, and they assured her that Mrs. Rubinstein was doing fine, they had only kept her there for the night so she wouldn't be alone at home. They had given her Vicodin for the considerable pain she was in, but there was no medical reason why she couldn't leave. For a woman her age, she was in remarkably good health, and had been fully coherent when she came in. The nurse on duty said she was a dear. Olympia agreed, and then called the for the thousandth time. After negotiating the blizzard again, her cold had gotten markedly worse.

"My mother? What's she doing here?" He looked confused.

"She broke her ankle. They took her to NYU in an ambulance, and she didn't even call me. I just picked her up half an hour ago."

"Are you serious?" He looked stunned.

"I am." She blew her nose yet again. "She can't stay at her place alone. She's in a cast and on crutches. I think she should stay here for a while."

Harry smiled lovingly at his wife. Olympia never let him down. "Is she awake?"

"She was a few minutes ago, but she's pretty looped on the stuff they gave her for the pain. Poor thing, it must have hurt like hell. I told her to call us on the intercom if she needs to, and not to try and go to the bathroom by herself. You know her. She'll be cooking us all breakfast in the morning. We're going to have to tie her to the bed."

"I'll go down and check on her," he said, looking concerned, and then turned to look at Olympia again as he headed out the door. "I love you. Thank you for being so good to her."

Olympia smiled back at him. "She's the only mom we've got."

"You're the best wife in the world."

"Shhh!" she said, putting a finger to her lips. "Don't say that!" He laughed at her, took a shower, and was in bed with her half an hour later. She was still blowing and coughing, and had just checked on Max. He was sound asleep.

"It looks like you're going to be running an infirmary here this week," Harry said as he snuggled up next to her, and put his arms around her. She had her back to him, so she didn't breathe on him, and it was comforting feeling him next to her.

"I'm sorry about your mom. That was rotten luck for her."

"She's lucky to have you, Ollie...so am I...don't think I don't appreciate all you do for her. You're an amazing woman."

"Thank you," she said, as she drifted off to sleep in his arms. "You're not so bad yourself."

"I'll try and come home early tomorrow," he promised. She nodded, and within seconds, was fast asleep.

always touched Olympia's heart. She tiptoed out of the room, and went back upstairs to take a shower. Harry was already nearly dressed. He had to be in the office for a press conference early that morning. And at seven, just as Olympia was combing her hair, Max woke up. He said he felt better, though he had as many spots as he'd had the night before, if not more.

"How are all your patients?" Harry asked as he put on his jacket and straightened his tie.

"Max says he feels better, and your mom is still asleep."

"Can you manage?" he asked, looking worried but also rushed.

Olympia laughed. "Do I have a choice?"

"I guess not," he said, looking apologetic. At least, he knew, now his mother going to the ball wouldn't be an issue. He had the excuse of staying home to take care of her, which he felt sure would get him off the hook, and make him look like less of a louse for not going. He had been feeling guilty about not going for weeks, but no matter how guilty he felt, he absolutely refused to go. And now his mother couldn't go, either. She could hardly go to a ball on crutches, unable to put any weight on one foot. He said nothing about it to his wife, but he was nonetheless relieved, although sorry about his mother's accident her briefcase, and literally ran out the door. There was a foot of fresh snow on the ground, but it had finally stopped falling. And as usual, in weather like that, it took her half an hour to find a cab. Margaret called her in the office that afternoon, and asked how things were going. All Olympia could do was laugh.

"Well, let's see, Max has chicken pox, Frieda broke her ankle yesterday and is staying in our den. I have the cold of the century. Ginny is sick at school. And Charlie's coming home tonight, thank God."

"Other than that, Mrs. Lincoln, how was the performance?"

"Yeah. Right. When it rains, it pours. I just hope the girls stay in one piece till Saturday. After that, we can all fall apart."

"What's Harry doing to help?"

"Nothing at the moment. He's dealing with a crisis at the court of appeals."

"I know. I saw his press conference this morning. Just when I'd decided I hate the guy for not going to the ball with you, I fell in love with him all over again for the positions he takes. The guy is really a mensch, even though I think he's an asshole for not going with you on Saturday."

"You can't have everything, I guess," Olympia said with a sigh. "I love him, too. He stands for the right stuff, and is willing to fight for it to the death.

cope with. As she pointed out regularly, she didn't even have pets or plants. Work was more than enough for her. And her husband was a dream. He took care of the house, organized their social life, and cooked for her when she got home. "Let me know if I can do anything to help," Margaret offered, but Olympia knew she had her hands full with her mother. She was just happy she'd be there Saturday night. With the girls nervous and wound up, Charlie and the other escort to keep track of, Frieda on crutches or in a wheelchair, and a potentially hostile ex-husband to deal with, Olympia was going to be crazed.

In spite of a new case that landed on her at four o'clock, Olympia left her office early, and managed to be home by five. Max was sitting on the couch in the den next to Frieda. She had her leg propped up on a chair, and Charlie was sitting with them, drinking tea, when Olympia walked in.

"Well, this looks like a cozy group. Hi, sweetheart," she said as she gave her son a big hug to welcome him home. She was visibly happy to have him back, and he looked equally pleased to see her. Max was still covered with calamine, but the doctor had assured them he was no longer contagious, so Frieda was enjoying his company, and had been all afternoon. Charlie had just gotten home, a few hours earlier than planned.

him to be careful and remember what had happened to Frieda. Charlie looked at her and smiled, and then left. Sometimes his mother still treated him like he was five.

Between running downstairs to check on Frieda, and putting Max to bed, cleaning up the kitchen, talking to Charlie, and taking a bath finally, Olympia didn't have time to talk to Harry alone until they were in bed that night.

"How did Charlie seem to you?" she asked, looking worried.

"Fine. Why? He seems to be having a great time playing hockey. And I think he's more relaxed about his future plans. He seemed uptight to me over Thanksgiving, but tonight I thought he was more laid-back."

"I can't put my finger on it. But I think something is still bothering him," she said with the finely tuned instincts of a mother.

"Did he say something to give you that impression?"

"No. He says he's fine. Maybe it's just my imagination, but I'm convinced something's on his mind."

"Stop looking for things to worry about," Harry chided her. "If he's upset, he'll tell you. Charlie's always good about that." Although he was private with others, he was exceptionally close to her.

better once he makes his mind up about whether to take the job in California, find a job here, go to divinity school, or go to Oxford. They're all good choices to have, but until he makes a decision, he'll probably be a nervous wreck." They both agreed that he seemed troubled.

"I think you're right. I remember how scared I was when I left college. I had no family to fall back on. I was terrified, and then I married Chauncey, and I thought I was home free after that. As it turned out, not as home free as I thought."

"You were too young to get married," Frieda said with a frown, although she had been younger than that herself when she married Harry's father. But things were different then, they had been through the war, survived the horror of the camps, and had led a different life. During the war, people grew up fast, particularly as she had. Her youth had ended in the concentration camp at Dachau.

"At least I got three great kids out of it," Olympia said philosophically, and Frieda smiled in response.

"Yes, you did. Charlie's a wonderful boy, and the girls are terrific, too." And then she looked at her daughter-in-law with a determined expression. "I'm still going to the ball, you know. I don't care what you say, I wouldn't miss it for the world." Olympia was sorry Harry didn't feel the same way. "Harry said I tears in her eyes as she said it. This was more than just a party for her. It was about being socially accepted in a way she never had been before. She had spent years of poverty, working in a sweatshop as a seamstress, beside her husband, to put their son through school. Just once before she died, she wanted to feel like Cinderella too, even if her son thought she was foolish. And she wanted to see her granddaughters make their debut. Olympia understood that, and vowed to make it happen for her. It was a dream come true for more than just the girls. It meant a lot to Frieda, too. More than Harry knew.

"We'll make it work, Frieda. I promise." The only thing Olympia couldn't figure out was who was going to push the wheelchair. She had to be at the hotel at five on Saturday to help the girls dress, and Charlie had to be there with them for rehearsal. There was no one to wheel her into the hotel, except Harry, who refused to go. She was thinking of asking Margaret and her husband to pick her up, if Olympia rented them all a limo. It was the only way to do it.

Olympia asked Harry about the ball cautiously again that night after dinner, and reminded him that with his mother disabled, the logistics of getting her there were going to be a lot harder than they would have been otherwise. She needed someone to help young girl, or an old woman. "I think this is really important to her," Olympia said gently.

"It shouldn't be," he said firmly. "And even if it is, I am a judge of the court of appeals. I can't endorse a discriminatory event just to please my mother, or my wife, or your daughters. I'm tired of being made to feel like an asshole about it, Ollie. I firmly believe in what I'm doing. I can't be there."

"I'm sure you wouldn't be the first Jew who has been a guest at The Arches. For all I know, there are even Jewish girls who've come out there."

"I doubt it. And even if that's true, I still have to take a position on this and stick to it. I don't think Martin Luther King ever went to a ball hosted by the Ku Klux Klan."

"Do you and Veronica have to boycott everything you don't believe in? I can't even buy groceries when she's home, without worrying about who I'm offending or persecuting. If I buy grapes, it's an affront to Cesar Chavez. If I buy South African goods, I'm disrespecting Nelson Mandela. Hell, half the time if I put on a sweater or a pair of shoes, or eat a piece of fruit in my own kitchen, I'm pissing someone off. It sure makes life complicated, and in this case, I think our family is more important than your goddamn political views. All your mother wants now is to go to a party to watch her stepgranddaughters make their

# Chapter 7

*Once the girls* came home from college, everything in the house was chaos. Their friends came and went, the phone rang constantly. Other girls who were making their debut at The Arches showed up to talk to Ginny, giggle, squeal, and take a peek at her dress. All the girls approved when they saw it. They all agreed it was gorgeous. Veronica holed up in her own room with her friends, none of whom were planning to come out.

Frieda left the door to the den open, and enjoyed watching the arrivals and departures. Olympia was bringing in kosher food for her, and Charlie helped her pick it up, and serve it to Frieda on separate dishes on trays. She had been extremely reasonable about not being quite as rigid about it as normal. She knew how complicated it was for Olympia to worry there. If not, she'd have to buy her a pair. Or Veronica was likely to do something crazy, like wear sneakers or red shoes. She let herself into the room as Veronica came out of the shower towel-drying her hair with her back to her mother. Olympia stopped in her tracks and stared at her in horror. Right in the center of her back was a giant tattoo. It was a huge multicolored butterfly with a wingspread the size of a dinner plate. Without even realizing it, Olympia screamed, and Veronica jumped about a foot, and wheeled around. She hadn't heard her mother come in.

"Oh my God! *What is that?*" She knew perfectly well what it was. She just couldn't believe that Veronica had done that to herself. It was huge. Olympia burst into tears.

"Come on, Mom...please...I'm sorry...I was going to tell you about it...I've always wanted to do it...I love it...you'll get used to it...." Veronica looked panicked. The one thing her mother had always forbidden them was piercings or tattoos. She had let them pierce their ears, but anywhere else was taboo. And tattoos were beyond the pale.

"I can't believe you did that!" Olympia said, sitting on the edge of Veronica's bed. She was feeling faint. Her baby's body had been desecrated. She couldn't even imagine Veronica living with that for the rest of her life. It was obscene. She wanted her to have it

"I'm not letting you come out at The Arches with that *thing* on your back." Ginny walked into the room as she said it, looking for a can of hairspray, saw her mother's devastated expression, and then looked at her twin.

Veronica spoke first. "Mom knows." Ginny looked uncomfortable to be caught between the two, and started to leave the room.

"You stay right here. If either of you ever gets another one, I'm killing you both. And that goes for Charlie, too."

"He'd never do it," Veronica reassured her. "He's too afraid to piss you off. So is Ginny."

"What makes you so brave?" Olympia asked miserably, blowing her nose in a tissue. She felt as though someone had died, although she knew it was only a tattoo.

"I figured you'd forgive me," Veronica said with a sheepish smile, and hugged her again, as her mother wiped her eyes.

"Don't be so sure. And we have to do something about the dress. I came in here to look for your shoes." They had shared such a wonderful Chanukah only hours before, and now there was this, to spoil it all for her.

"I can't find my shoes," Veronica admitted blithely. "I think I gave them away."

exchange. Was this your revenge for making you come out? The iron butterfly?"

"No, Mom," Veronica said, looking unhappy. "I got it the first week of school, as a symbol of my independence and flying free. My metamorphosis into being an adult."

"Wonderful. I guess I'm lucky you didn't put a caterpillar on there too, to show the before and after." She stood up then and looked at both her daughters, and without another word, she left the room. She passed Harry on the stairs and didn't say a word to him. She went downstairs to the kitchen and made herself a cup of tea. He could see how upset she was, and thought it was still about him. It was after midnight, and Olympia was obviously severely overwrought.

Frieda saw her walk past her open door with her head down, and a few minutes later hobbled into the kitchen on her crutches. Olympia was sitting at the kitchen table, crying over her cup of tea. She was thinking about the backless dress and what they were going to do. More than that, she was thinking about Veronica's perfect young body, and how she had defaced it. It would never be the same.

"Uh-oh," Frieda said, looking at her. She'd had a feeling something was wrong, which was why she had come in. It wasn't like Olympia not to stick her head in the door to see how she was. "What's wrong?"

was bright red from blowing it all week. At least the antibiotics had helped Ginny. She was much better by the time she got home. Olympia could hardly say the words as she looked across the table at her mother-in-law. "She got a tattoo."

"A tattoo?" Frieda looked stunned. It hadn't even occurred to her. On a list of possible tragedies, it would have been last on her list. "Where?"

"In the middle of her back," Olympia said miserably. "This big!" She framed her hands to indicate the size of it all too accurately.

"Oh dear," Frieda said, digesting the information Olympia had shared with her. "That's not good. What a foolish thing to do. I know they're fashionable now, but she'll be sorry she did it one day."

"She's thrilled with it," Olympia said unhappily. "I have to get her a new dress tomorrow. She can't wear the one she has. I have to get her one now with a high back. Or a stole. I'm not sure what kind of miracle I can pull off in a day." And she was still feeling sick.

Frieda looked thoughtful for a moment, and nodded. "Get me four yards of white satin tomorrow, good stuff, not the cheesy synthetics. I'll make a stole for her. She can wear it for the presentation at least. After that, well... after that it's up to her and you. Would she wear a stole?" Frieda looked as worried as to faint when I saw that thing on her back. She had just gotten out of the shower. I guess she's been hiding it for months."

"It could be worse. It could be a skull and crossbones, or some boy's name she won't remember by next year. How's Ginny's romance, by the way? Is the boy still coming?"

"Tomorrow night apparently, and she says it's okay. Veronica doesn't like him, and she has pretty good judgment about men, better than Ginny. I hope he's a nice kid. She's all excited about his seeing her in her gown."

"It's all so sweet," Frieda said, looking starry-eyed, "and don't worry, we'll cover the tattoo. No one will know except us." It was lovely having a mother-in-law who wanted to solve problems and not cause them. Olympia knew that was rare and appreciated her enormously. She was more like her own mother than Harry's.

Olympia told Harry about the tattoo when she went to bed, and he was as upset as she was. Defacing one's body was not only against his aesthetic principles, but also against his religion. He could just imagine how Olympia felt. She was still upset about it early the next morning when she went out to buy the white satin. Afterward, she went to Manolo Blahnik to buy the white satin shoes, and had

They were all getting ready to go to bed, when Olympia heard Ginny come in. There were voices in the downstairs hall, outside Frieda's room, the sound of running on the stairs, and then Olympia saw her fly past her open door and heard her sobbing.

"Uh-oh." She looked at Harry. "Trouble in River City. I'll be back." She went down the hall to Ginny's room and found her lying on the bed, crying uncontrollably. It took her mother nearly ten minutes to find out what was wrong. Steve had arrived from Providence that night, gone to dinner with her, and told her that he had actually come to New York to tell her it was over. He dumped her, and already had another girlfriend. Ginny was beside herself. She was crazy about him. Olympia couldn't help wondering why he had come to New York to deliver the message in person the night before her big event. He couldn't tell her afterward, or even on the phone? It seemed like a nasty stunt to her, and a devastating one to Ginny. There was little she could say to console her.

"I'm sorry, sweetheart...I'm so sorry...it was a rotten thing to do...." It didn't seem fair to tell her she'd forget about him and there would be another thousand men in her life, after him. Right now it felt like a mortal blow, and a cruel trick.

"I'm not going tomorrow...," Ginny said in muffled tones into the mattress. "I can't....I don't care much pain on her baby. All she could do now was help pick up the pieces.

It was nearly midnight when she got back to her own room. Ginny was miserable but calm again. She had finally stopped crying. And Harry was sound asleep. Olympia lay in bed next to him, closed her eyes, and silently prayed. . . . Please God, let everyone stay sane tomorrow and behave decently tomorrow night. . . . I can't take any more surprises. . . . Please God, just for one night. . . . Thank you, God. . . . Goodnight. And with that, she fell asleep.

and Frieda wished her luck for that night. She asked if there was anything she could do to help, but as far as Olympia knew, everything was in order. Both girls were still asleep. Harry had gone out early to play squash at his club. Max was feeling better. Charlie had spent the night with friends. For the moment, the house was peaceful.

At eleven o'clock, Ginny woke up and came rushing downstairs with a look of panic. She found her mother in Frieda's room, exploded into the room, and announced, "I lost a glove!" One of the long white ones, presumably, that were mandatory to wear. Her mother looked calm.

"No, you didn't. I saw them both yesterday. They were on top of your dresser, with your bag."

Ginny looked instantly uncomfortable and slightly guilty. "I took them to Debbie's last night, to show her how gorgeous they were, and then everything happened with Steve. I forgot one of them there. She said the dog chewed it to bits last night."

"Oh for God's sake..." Olympia struggled not to get upset. "When am I supposed to get another pair?... All right, all right... I'll go, now before I take you to the hairdresser. I hope they have another pair in your size." Frieda watched with enormous admiration as Olympia handled the situation with aplomb. Ten minutes later Olympia was wearing jeans, a ski had no other choice. Her mother was feeling rotten. Olympia said she understood, and stood staring at the phone for a minute, trying to figure it out. She had to be at the hotel with the girls from five o'clock on. Charlie had to be there by four, which left no one to accompany Frieda in the limousine. She had an idea then, and went to discuss it with Harry.

He listened carefully, convinced she was going to try and manipulate him into going with her at the last minute. She had given up all hope of that. All she wanted from him was to get his mother into the limousine, put the wheelchair in with her, and call Olympia on her cell phone the minute they left the house. Olympia would then go down to the lobby and out to the street, meet Frieda in the limousine, put her in the wheelchair, and get her upstairs to dinner before the ball. Olympia made it sound easy. The fact that she'd be dressing two hysterical girls, watching them be photographed, and trying to calm them down, while dressing herself, she didn't mention to her husband.

"Can you do that for me?" she asked after outlining her plan for his mother.

"Of course I can. She's my mother." Olympia made no comment about his not going with them, nor asked him to join her. All she wanted was for him to get his mother into the limousine and call her. They he understood, and sounded very quiet. He promised to wake his mother at six o'clock, and would help her dress. The limousine was coming for her at seven-fifteen. There was a dinner for the girls, their escorts, and their families. The rest of the guests were coming at nine. Rehearsal was at five. It was in the same ballroom as the ball was held. Olympia got the girls downstairs on schedule, at ten to five.

As it so happened, Veronica's escort, Jeff Adams, was walking in, with his tailcoat on a hanger, just as Olympia and the girls appeared at the entrance to the ballroom for rehearsal. Olympia closed her eyes, hoping she was hallucinating. As it turned out, she wasn't. Jeff Adams had bright blue hair. Not dark blue, or midnight blue, which might be mistaken for black in a darkened ballroom. It was somewhere between turquoise and sapphire, and there was no mistaking what color it was, in any light. He looked extremely pleased with himself, and insufferably arrogant as he shook Olympia's hand. Veronica looked at him and laughed. Ginny still looked like a zombie, after Steve's perfidy of the night before. He had told her that even though he was dumping her for another girl, he was "willing" to come to the ball. And much to Olympia's horror, Ginny had told him he could. She said she wanted one last night with him. Thinking about it made Olympia feel sick, but she new phase of her life. It was no longer enough to throw out the grapes her mother bought, now apparently she had to shock everyone and make a spectacle of herself. Olympia was far from pleased.

She mentioned it to her when they went back to their room after rehearsal, to dress.

"Veronica, that wasn't funny. All he did was make the members of the committee mad at him, and you by association."

"Come on, Mom, don't be so uptight. If we have to do something as dumb as this, we might as well have a sense of humor about it."

"It wasn't humorous," Olympia insisted. "It was rude and annoying. Is he going to dye it back?"

"Of course he is. He just did it to be funny."

"He wasn't." Olympia looked seriously aggravated, and by then, Ginny was crying again. She had just heard from Steve on her cell phone. He was no longer sure he was coming. He thought it might be too hard for her. Ginny told him between sobs that it would be harder if he didn't. She damn near begged him, while Olympia cringed listening to her, and finally he agreed to come. If Olympia's thoughts of him could have killed him, the infamous Steve would have been dead on the spot. Instead, he was going to be her dinner guest, and break her daughter's heart on one of the most important nights of her life.

"I don't know. I think I'm more nervous than the girls. They both look gorgeous. They're having photographs taken right now. I have to join them as soon as your mother comes. Chauncey and Felicia are probably already downstairs." She wasn't looking forward to that.

She didn't tell Harry that she missed him, because she didn't want to make him feel guiltier than she already had. There was no point. It hadn't gotten her anywhere. She had a brief fantasy that he was in the limousine with her mother-in-law, but she could hear from the sound of Max talking in the background that Harry was obviously still at home. This was just going to be one of those disappointments that happened in a marriage, that she would have to swallow and forget. There were lots of other things he did right. And other than this, he had always been there for her, and would be again. This was one thing he couldn't do for her, and that she had no choice but to accept. There was no point damaging their relationship over a coming-out ball he wouldn't attend. She couldn't allow it to mean that much. She said good-bye to him hurriedly, left the room, and took the elevator downstairs. She was waiting on the street for Frieda, shivering, when her limousine arrived. Frieda looked like a dignified grande dame in her elegant black dress, with her hair swept into a smooth French twist she sure she would have been capable of it herself. She was furious with her son, for letting Olympia down. But before she could say more about it, a tall blond man in white tie and tails approached them, with an equally tall blond woman at his side. It was Chauncey and Felicia. Olympia introduced them to Frieda. Felicia said good evening to Frieda politely, Chauncey ignored her entirely while he greeted his ex-wife. In spite of the fact that she'd dressed quickly, and paid little attention to herself, Olympia looked spectacular that night. Chauncey looked her over with a practiced air.

"You're looking well, Olympia," he said, kissing her cheek. She thanked him, and shook hands with Felicia, who looked silly in a pink satin dress that was way too low and way too tight. Olympia was startled to notice that she looked cheap. She didn't remember her looking that way, but it had been years since they last met. She hadn't improved with age. And she could see that the girls' unflattering comments about her were right. She looked foolish, and dressed inappropriately for her age. Olympia's well-cut navy blue satin evening gown looked more elegant, much sexier, and wasn't nearly as low cut. Olympia looked spectacular and dignified. Chauncey seemed to notice it, too. He put an arm around her shoulders, and gave her a hug "for old times' sake." Looking at him, grateful for small mercies. Jeff glanced at her with a look of supercilious amusement, and she had a powerful urge to slap him. He was arrogance personified, although admittedly a handsome kid, but the kind of boy who thought he was smarter than everyone, especially anyone's parents. She couldn't help wondering if Veronica had invited him to upset her. She had done everything else possible to do so since Olympia and Chauncey had forced her to make her debut. Veronica was doing it, but no one was going to force her to take it seriously, or enjoy it. And Ginny was still looking upset when both girls kissed their father, and said hello to Felicia. She told the girls they looked beautiful, and Frieda cried when she hugged them.

After family photographs, the girls, their escorts, and the girls' families all went to another floor for dinner. Olympia was sitting between Veronica and Frieda. Chauncey and Felicia were next to Ginny. Everything seemed to be going perfectly, until Chauncey got up to go to the men's room, halfway through dinner. Veronica had draped her stole over the back of her chair. It was too awkward to manage during dinner, in the slippery satin. She and her mother had momentarily forgotten why she had worn it in the first place. Chauncey stopped directly behind her chair and looked as if he'd been shot. He turned directly toward his ex-wife and stared at her in disbelief.

you're going to disfigure yourself in that way, you belong in prison, with other people who look like you." Olympia was momentarily terrified that Veronica would tell him to go fuck himself, and cause a bigger scene than they already had. Everyone was riveted by the scene. He wasn't subtle, and thanks to the booze he'd already consumed, he was loud. Even Felicia looked surprised by the fuss he was making.

"I'm not going to discuss this with you, Dad. Why don't you grow up?" Veronica said, standing up and looking him in the eye. "It's a tattoo, not a crime. Why don't you have another drink? I'm sure that will make you feel better," she said in icy tones, and then walked out of the room. Jeff saw her leave, and followed her out. As she disappeared, everyone at the table got a full view of the tattoo Chauncey was objecting to so loudly. Felicia turned to look and gasped. She assured everyone at the table that none of her own daughters would think of doing a thing like that, and then admitted that her oldest daughter was just thirteen. Olympia knew that a lot was due to change in Felicia's life in the next five years. In spite of one's best efforts, there was only so much one could do to control one's kids.

Olympia didn't like it either, but much to her surprise, she thought Veronica had handled the scene with dignity and decorum, far more so than her less gown. I think in her day everyone had to wear little cap sleeves to cover their arms. It's just the way things are today."

"I guess you're right," Olympia said, finally calming down. She could see that Chauncey was still fuming when he resumed his seat. He glared across the table at his ex-wife, while Frieda watched him with an anxious frown.

"That's the most outrageous thing I've ever seen," Chauncey said more quietly this time. By then, Felicia knew what it was about.

"I don't like it either," Olympia said to Chauncey quietly after he sat down. "She had it done while she was at school. I just discovered it this week."

"You're far too liberal with that child, with all of them in fact. She'll wind up in jail as a Communist one of these days," he said, as he ordered another drink.

"They don't put Communists in jail, Chauncey. She's liberal, but she's not totally out of her mind. She just wants to prove she has her own ideas."

"That's no way to do it," he said with a look of outraged disapproval. Veronica's tattoo had shocked him to the core.

"No, it isn't. I hate to say it, but I suppose it's harmless. Ugly, but harmless." Olympia was resigning

The meal was over, and it was time to go back up-stairs and join their guests in the ballroom. The girls were going to form a receiving line, to greet the guests as they went in, while their escorts waited for them backstage. It was nearly nine o'clock.

was no longer married to him. Whatever Harry's faults, he was an intelligent, kind, decent man.

Once on the ballroom floor again, they went through the receiving line. It seemed to take forever, and Frieda sat and beamed at the girls when they got to them. She and Olympia had shaken all fifty properly extended gloved right hands. There were some very pretty girls in the group, but none as pretty, Olympia thought, as her twins. They looked dazzling in the very different but equally beautiful white evening gowns.

Frieda was still smiling with pride and pleasure when they found their table. Olympia settled her in, and sat down next to her. Ginny's friend Steve was already sitting there. He stood up politely and introduced himself, looking faintly embarrassed, and then sat down again. Olympia was cool and still seriously annoyed at him. The other couple she had invited came shortly afterward. She introduced them to Frieda, and within seconds Margaret Washington and her husband appeared. She had left her mother at the hospital in good hands. She was wearing a spectacular brown lace gown, almost the same color as her skin. Frieda thought she looked like a young Lena Horne. It was a congenial group as everyone talked about how beautiful the girls had looked on the receiving line.

Chauncey wanted, and stayed home. Olympia had brought the real world right into the ball with her, a Holocaust survivor and a brilliant young black lawyer who had grown up in Harlem. What better way to prove the point to them? She could think of none.

As she thought about it, she was startled to see Charlie walk toward her across the ballroom, and wondered if something was wrong. Everyone was at their table by then, and the girls had gone backstage to get ready for the presentation. Noses were being powdered, hair was being smoothed down and combed, lipstick was being put on. The band had begun to play, and the debutantes' parents and friends were dancing. They had another twenty minutes to enjoy themselves before the show began. Charlie strode purposefully across the floor, and much to his mother's surprise, he asked her to dance. She smiled at him, touched by the gesture. She knew he had done it because Harry wasn't there. And he knew how hard it was for her to spend an evening with his father. He had been boorish to her about the tattoo and rude to her guests. And for some odd reason, Chauncey and Felicia had invited none of their own. Charlie led his mother out on the dance floor, among the other parents, and began a graceful fox trot with her.

"Have I told you lately how proud I am of you?" She looked up at her firstborn with a happy smile,

"I know this is a crazy place to do it, Mom. And I know it's probably the wrong time. But I've wanted to tell you something for a while."

"If you tell me you have a skull and crossbones tattooed on your chest, I'm going to hit you." He laughed and shook his head, and his eyes grew serious again.

"No, Mom. I'm gay." He didn't miss a step as he danced with her, and she looked at him with eyes filled with more love and pride than he had ever dared to hope he would see there once he told her. She hadn't let him down. And for her, the question she'd seen in his eyes for so long had finally been answered. She didn't say anything for a long time, and then she leaned closer to him and kissed him.

"I love you, Charlie. Thank you for telling me." His confidence in her was the greatest gift he could have given her, just as her peaceful acceptance of what he had told her was the greatest gift she could have given him. "I guess when I think about it, I'm not all that surprised. I am, but I'm not. Was that what happened with the boy who killed himself last year? Were you in love with him?" Maybe in her heart of hearts she had wondered about it all along. She was no longer sure. Maybe her heart had told her Charlie was different long before her head understood.

"No." He shook his head. "We were just friends. He

"I think Harry will be fine. In fact, I'm sure of it. Tell him whenever you want."

"I will. Thanks, Mom," he said then, looking down at her. He looked happier than she'd seen him in months. And as she looked at him, the dance came to an end. "You're the best mom anyone could ever have. Now can I tell you about the tattoo on my back?" He laughed at her, looking like a kid again. But that night they both knew he had become a man. He had taken the terrifying step from childhood into adulthood. Tonight had been a rite of passage for him, too, a terrifying one. And thanks to her, he had landed on both feet, and the ground under him was solid, whatever his sexual preferences were. She loved him no matter what. That was clear. He had her unconditional love and respect.

"Don't you dare tell me you have a tattoo, Charlie Walker. I might have to strangle you for that!"

"Don't worry, Mom, I don't." He had to go back-stage to the others then, but he had known that before he did, he had to tell her. He didn't know why, but he knew that he had to tell her tonight. He wanted to. In a different way than his sisters, he had come out, too.

She turned to look at him again before he led her back to her table, and she told him just what he wanted to hear and needed from her. "I'm proud of you." He kissed her cheek and led her back to her

And then he laughed. "My mother told me tonight when she left that she was ashamed of me. She said I was the most prejudiced person she knew. Max even said it was stupid of me not to come. I know it was. The only one I care about here is you, and the kids of course. But I wanted to be here with you. I'm sorry I let you come here alone. How was dinner, by the way?"

"Interesting. Chauncey had a tantrum over Veronica's tattoo. I don't blame him, but as usual, he went a little overboard."

"Did she tell him to get fucked?" he asked with amusement. He had obviously missed the fireworks over dinner, but had turned up for the best part, the part that really mattered to her. The presentation of her girls to society, whatever that was.

"Remarkably, she didn't," she said in answer to his question about what Veronica had said to her father. "She told him to grow up. That's not a bad idea. Getting sober wouldn't be a bad idea, either. He still drinks too much." She had a lot of things to tell him when they went home that night, mostly Charlie's admission to her. It was foremost in her mind. But she didn't want to tell him here. She was still a little startled by what her son had told her, but touched that he had taken her into his confidence at last. He had looked like a thousand-pound weight had been lifted off his shoulders from the moment he told her. She a spotlight shone on an arch of flowers. A line of cadets from West Point appeared, raised their sabers, and crossed them. The debutantes were going to pass underneath, just as they had when Olympia made her debut twenty-seven years before. Frieda's eyes were wide as she watched the performance, and a moment later, the first girl came out. They appeared alphabetically, and Olympia knew that with the last name of Walker, the twins were going to come out last. They had forty-eight other girls to watch before Virginia and Veronica made their bows.

The girls came out slowly, some looking nervous, others looking confident, some smiling broadly, others not at all. The wreaths of flowers on their heads made them look almost angelic, and some of the gowns were really lovely, others were slightly over the top. There were fat girls and thin ones, exquisite ones and plain ones, but as each of them came out, holding her bouquet, her gloved hand tucked into her escort's arm, each looked as though it was the most glorious moment of her life. The announcer called their names, and those of their escorts. They stood still, as everyone applauded, siblings whistled and shouted, and with measured grace, they curtsied, walked slowly down the stairs and under the cadets' sabers, and crossed the ballroom to wait for the others. There was something slightly silly about it, and young beauties, curtsied one last time, and then the fathers were invited to come to the dance floor. Chauncey got up more steadily than Olympia expected, and walked proudly onto the dance floor to claim Virginia. Olympia then whispered something to Harry. He hesitated, and she nodded, and then he went out to claim Veronica.

Chauncey glanced at him for a moment, and then nodded. As though prearranged, they each danced with one girl for half a dance, and then switched. It was a moment Olympia knew that she, Harry, and Frieda would never forget. The man who had objected so strenuously to everything the evening stood for had danced with her daughters the night of their debut. And when the dance was over, much to Olympia's amazement, Chauncey shook his hand. It had turned out to be a rite of passage not only for the children but for the adults as well. Both families had acknowledged their bond to each other through their children. And then Chauncey came back to the table and invited Olympia to dance.

"I still haven't gotten over that tattoo," he said, looking down at her, smiling this time. For an instant, she could almost remember the man she had once loved. He shared these lovely children with her, and they had just shared a night that they would all long remember and cherish. She laughed at what he said.

cast, she would have danced all night. She said it was the most magical evening of her life. Just seeing how thrilled she was to have been there touched Harry's and Olympia's hearts.

Charlie had made a point of coming to say goodbye to them before he left with the girls. They were going to a private club to dance some more. It was a night none of them would ever forget. Charlie had whispered to his mother before he left, "Thanks again, Mom, I love you."

"I love you, too, sweetheart." She smiled at him. For that one night, everything that mattered bonded them to each other. Both girls had come to thank her. Even Veronica said she'd had a great time, which was exactly what Harry said as they left.

"I had a terrific time, Ollie," he said, looking at her tenderly. He loved what she had done for his mother. She had known instinctively how much it meant to Frieda, and nothing in the world could have stopped Olympia from getting her there. Each in their own way, they had all come out that night. Perhaps Harry most of all. He had given up his radical ideals for just a moment, allowed himself to be mellowed, and discovered that it wasn't such a travesty to move in many worlds. Frieda's eyes were still sparkling as they got in the limousine. Tonight Frieda was Cinderella, good night, then she turned off the light and left the room. Harry was waiting for her in the hallway outside his mother's room. They walked upstairs hand in hand and quietly closed the door to their bedroom, so they didn't wake Max. The sitter Harry had called at the last minute had left when they got home. She'd been fast asleep in Charlie's room, since it was nearly three. It was almost four when Harry unzipped Olympia's dress and looked at her with pleasure, and then she remembered what she hadn't been able to tell him until then. Her eyes grew serious as she looked at him.

"Charlie told me something very important tonight."

"That he has a tattoo, too?" he teased, and she shook her head. She wasn't sad for Charlie. She had enormous respect for him.

"Charlie came out tonight, too."

"Out of what?" Harry asked, looking confused, and then he understood. It didn't completely surprise him, although he had never been sure. But he had wondered once or twice, and didn't want to say anything to Olympia, in case his suspicions weren't accurate. He was afraid it might upset her. It hadn't. It had surprised her, but she loved him more than ever.

"He told me," she said proudly. She was touched

and strangers became friends. Just as she had said it would be, it was a rite of passage, and a lovely tradition, and nothing more. It was a night when he had come out from an old world into a new one, when others got a glimpse backward into an old one. When the past and future met in one shining moment, when time stopped, sadness slipped away and was forgotten, and life began.

## About the Author

DANIELLE STEEL has been hailed as one of the world's most popular authors, with over 590 million copies of her novels sold. Her many international bestsellers include *Southern Lights, Matters of the Heart, One Day at a Time, A Good Woman, Rogue, Honor Thyself, Amazing Grace, Bungalow 2,* and other highly acclaimed novels. She is also the author of *His Bright Light,* the story of her son Nick Traina's life and death.

www.daniellesteel.com.